D0349395
WATERFORD CITY AND COUNTY LIBRARIES
WITHDRAWN

With thanks to Poppy and Fuchsia,
for sharing their family with me – J. H.

To Poppy H. – J. B.

First published 2004 by Walker Books Ltd
87 Vauxhall Walk, London SE11 5HJ

10 9 8 7 6 5 4 3 2 1

This book has been typeset in Giovanni

Printed in China

British Library Cataloguing in Publication Data:
a catalogue record for this book is available from the British Library

ISBN 0-7445-6728-9

www.walkerbooks.co.uk

Judy Hindley

What's in Baby's Morning?

ILLUSTRATED BY Jo Burroughes

WALKER BOOKS
AND SUBSIDIARIES
LONDON • BOSTON • SYDNEY • AUCKLAND

What's in Baby's morning?

A sister sleeping –
just over there –
counting-beads
and little chair,
Spotty Dog
and Mrs Cow
and Little Hup
the hippo.

"Good morning,
Little Hup!"

And here's a mother

who picks him up,

gives him a kiss,

gives him a hug,

finds his clothes

and puts them on,

with a sock and a shoe

for each little foot,

and a hat for Little Hup.

"There you go, Little Hup!"

What's in Baby's morning?

Breakfast bowl

and bib and cup.

A sister who hides

to make him laugh.

Peep-bo, there she goes, popping down …
and up again – with a "BOO!" for Little Hup!

Now what's in Baby's morning?

A trailer that's red,

and a toddle truck.

A very kind father

who loads it up

with Spotty Dog

and Mrs Cow,

counting-beads

and alphabet blocks,

and Little Hup on top.

"Hold on, Little Hup!"

And there they go riding
round and round,
with shadows of leaves
skipping over the ground,

bug on a finger, juice in a cup,

tickly grass when shoes come off.

Then it's up and up to the birds and the sun,

and round and round and down again.

But then – oh, no!

Sobs and wails! Roars and howls!
Slippery tears all down Baby's face. He can't find Little Hup!

"Where are you, Little Hup?"

Here!

Little Hup is back!

So what's in Baby's morning now?

A happy smile
all over his face,
a time to say
"Hurray, hurray!"
and a special kiss
for his sister,
for finding
Little Hup.
"Be good now,
Little Hup!"

And this is how
the morning ends.

A drink, a cuddle,
a storybook,
heavy eyes
and sleepy yawn.
A mother who
tucks her baby up,
for a comfy nap
with Mrs Cow
and Spotty Dog

and Little Hup the hippo.

Shh! Hush, everyone!
Baby's going for a nap.

Sweet dreams, Baby!

Sweet dreams,

Little Hup!